# DATA IS THE NEW OIL

FARHAN SHARIEFF

WITH CHETAN S. BATRA

NOTION PRESS

NOTION PRESS

TITLE: DATA IS THE NEW OIL

ISBN: 9798895449981



First Edition: September, 2024

Cover Design: Chetan S. Batra

*This book is dedicated to-*

My Parents

Firdous & Nayeem

Security & Privacy Network

# WORD OF THANKS

This book is a culmination of the unwavering support, guidance, and encouragement I have received from many incredible people throughout my journey.

First and foremost, my deepest gratitude goes to my family. Your love, belief, and endless patience have been the foundation upon which this work is built.

To my friends and colleagues, thank you for your insightful conversations and honest feedback. Your perspectives challenged me to think critically and creatively, shaping the direction of this book.

I would like to express my heartfelt thanks to Mr. Stany Pereira for giving me the platform to grow in the fields of Cybersecurity & Privacy in the UAE. Your trust has been instrumental in my development.

I am also deeply grateful to Mr. Shaji Joseph for supporting me throughout my journey in the UAE. This incredible opportunity has allowed me to grow both personally and professionally. Your faith in my abilities has been a driving force behind this work, and I am forever thankful.

A special mention goes to Mr. Gaurav Shukla, whose mentorship has been invaluable. Your wisdom, advice, and constant encouragement have not only shaped this book but have had a lasting impact on my personal and professional growth. I am incredibly fortunate to have had the opportunity to learn from you.

I would also like to thank Mr. Hoshedar Cooper and Mr. Shajan Abraham for their support and motivation. Your insightful advice have profoundly impacted both this book and my personal development.

To my colleagues Mr.Nadim Shaikh and Mr.Ashish Joshi, I owe a special debt of gratitude for your contributions and support.

A heartfelt thanks to the entire team—Lalit, Divyank, Viraj, Anmol and Kashish—for your encouragement and camaraderie.

My deepest thanks to Chetan and Shashwat for their support and encouragement. Your friendship and insights have been incredible to me throughout this journey.

Lastly, to the readers, thank you for embarking on this journey with me. I hope that the stories, ideas, and insights within these pages resonate with you and bring you as much joy in reading as I experienced in writing them.

# CONTENTS

# FOREWORD

Data: The New Oil

With great pleasure, I write this foreword for Farhan
Sharieff's insightful and timely book, "Data is the New
Oil." Farhan was a brilliant and dedicated professional
during his time as my colleague, and I had the privilege of
mentoring him as he developed his skills in the field of
data privacy management and security.

Farhan's book offers a captivating and informative
exploration of the critical role that data plays in our
modern world. With a keen eye for detail and a deep
understanding of the subject matter, Farhan guides us
through a series of thrilling adventures that highlight the
challenges and opportunities presented by the digital age.

Farhan's writing is engaging and thought-provoking, from
the perilous depths of the dark web to the high-stakes
battles for control of blockchain technology. His ability to
weave complex technical concepts into compelling
narratives makes this book accessible to readers of all
backgrounds.

As we navigate the ever-evolving landscape of data,
Farhan's book serves as a valuable resource for anyone
seeking to understand the challenges and opportunities

that lie ahead. I am confident that readers will find "Data is the New Oil: Security & Privacy are the refineries" to be both informative and inspiring.

I commend Farhan for his excellent work on this book and wish him continued success in his future endeavors.

Kirti Kumar Salunke
Head of IT Risk Advisory
MGC Global Risk Advisory LLP
Certified CISM, ITIL Expert, PRINCE2 Practitioner, COBIT5, TOGAF, ISO 27001 Lead Implementor, Lean Six Sigma Green Belt, Data Protection Officer (DPO)

# CHAPTER ONE: INTRODUCING THE DIGITAL SENTINELS

Just as crude oil needs refining to become valuable, raw data must be processed, protected, and secured to unlock its true potential. In the digital world, where threats lurk at every corner, this refining process is crucial. The "Digital Sentinels," known for their legendary exploits in the cyber realm, now find themselves on a different kind of mission—a cyber voyage against the digital pirates of Cloud Island.

Each member of the crew brings their unique abilities to the table, taking on specialized roles in their epic battle against cyber threats and data thieves. Together, they form an unbreakable defense, ensuring that their data is as secure as the legendary treasure they seek.

1.  Captain Leo Strong – Captain and Frontline Defender
    As the captain, Leo leads the crew with his indomitable will and unyielding strength. In the cyber realm, he embodies the role of the primary security enforcer, using his power and creativity to fend off direct cyber-attacks. Just as he protects his crew in battle, Leo shields their systems, deploying powerful encryption techniques that act like a barrier, repelling any

threats that dare to breach their defenses. His leadership ensures the crew remains united and focused on their mission to protect and reclaim stolen data.

2. Blade Zane – Security Enforcer
Zane, the swordsman with unyielding resolve, slices through malware and digital threats with the same precision he uses to cut down enemies. As the crew's Security Enforcer, Zane is the guardian of their critical systems, standing firm against any digital onslaught. His expertise ensures that only those with proper authorization can access sensitive information, and his vigilance keeps their systems free from compromise.

3. Nina Wave – Navigator and Network Security Specialist
Nina, the skilled navigator, guides the crew through the treacherous waters of cyberspace. Her role as the Network Security Specialist involves charting a safe course through potential digital threats, ensuring that their data flows securely across networks. With her ability to control the flow of information, she creates a secure digital environment, using encryption to protect their data as it's transmitted. Nina's expertise ensures the crew can navigate safely, even in the stormiest of cyber seas.

4. Ace Sharp – Ethical Hacker and Cyber Defense Specialist
Ace, the crew's sharpshooter, becomes the Ethical Hacker, targeting vulnerabilities in the enemy's systems with precision. His role is to

test and reinforce the crew's defenses, ensuring they are prepared for any cyber assault. Ace's technical prowess allows him to craft unique tools and strategies, turning the tide of battle in their favor. Whether it's developing exploits to breach enemy defenses or setting up traps to neutralize threats, Ace ensures the crew's systems are always one step ahead.

5.  Saul Ember – Data Privacy Officer and Encryption Specialist
    Saul, the cook who cherishes the privacy of his recipes, takes on the mantle of Data Privacy Officer. He ensures that all data handled by the crew is as secure as a treasured secret. Saul's encryption techniques are the finest, wrapping their data in layers of security that only the most skilled could hope to penetrate. His commitment to privacy extends beyond the crew, ensuring that any data recovered is treated with the utmost confidentiality.

6.  Chip Doc – Incident Response and Cyber Health Specialist
    Chip, the crew's doctor, becomes the guardian of their cyber health. As the Incident Response Specialist, he monitors the crew's systems for any signs of infection or compromise. Chip's keen eye detects anomalies, allowing him to act swiftly to contain and remedy threats. Just as he heals the crew from physical wounds, Chip applies his "cyber medicine" to restore their systems to full health after an attack.

7. Raven Noir – Forensic Analyst and Threat Intelligence Specialist
   Raven, the investigator who uncovers the secrets of the past, now digs deep into the digital realm. As the Forensic Analyst, she uncovers the hidden tactics used by their enemies, providing the crew with crucial intelligence. Raven's analysis ensures that they understand the threats they face, allowing them to anticipate and counter enemy strategies. Her gathered intelligence is the key to staying one step ahead of the Cloud Pirates.

8. Steel Forge – Chief Information Security Officer (CISO) and Cyber Defense Engineer
   Steel, the engineer who builds their cyber fortress, constructs the crew's defenses. As the CISO, Steel designs and implements robust security architectures that protect their systems from even the most sophisticated attacks. His engineering skills are unmatched, creating defenses that are as impenetrable as a fortress. Steel's innovations keep the crew's data secure, allowing them to sail confidently into the unknown.

9. Echo Strings – Security Awareness Trainer and Backup Specialist
   Echo, the musician who knows the value of a well-rehearsed tune, becomes the Security Awareness Trainer. He ensures that the crew is educated on the latest cybersecurity best practices, so they know how to recognize and respond to threats. Echo also oversees their backup and recovery processes, ensuring that no data is lost and that recovery is swift in the event

of an attack. His efforts keep the crew prepared and their data safe, even in the face of adversity.

10. Tide Force – Zero Trust Architect and Access Control Specialist
Tide, the helmsman with a deep sense of honor, takes charge as the Zero Trust Architect. He implements a security model where trust is earned, not given. Tide ensures that access to the crew's systems is tightly controlled, with every action scrutinized. His architecture leaves no room for complacency, as every access request is verified, ensuring that only those with legitimate needs can enter the crew's digital domain.

# CHAPTER TWO: THE CALL TO ADVENTURE

In the heart of the cyber seas, where data streams flow endlessly and encrypted codes hold promises of untold secrets, the Digital Sentinels embarked on yet another daring voyage. This time, their quest led them to the mystical Isle of Cybersia, a land shrouded in digital mysteries and guarded by enigmatic forces.

The crew, though seasoned by many cyber adventures, faced a new kind of challenge—one that transcended the physical dangers of the digital realm and delved deep into the intricacies of cybersecurity. As they approached Cybersia, the island's silhouette appeared against the twilight sky, resembling a massive data server brimming with encrypted secrets.

Captain Leo Strong, the fearless leader, stood at the helm, his eyes gleaming with excitement. "Alright, Digital Sentinels! We've navigated through the toughest firewalls and bypassed the trickiest security protocols. Now, we face something entirely new—data security and privacy on an unprecedented scale. This is going to be our greatest adventure yet!"

The crew disembarked and was immediately greeted by an array of digital constructs, their forms both familiar and strange. The island's landscape was dotted with towering firewalls and complex algorithms, creating an environment that was as much a labyrinth of technology as it was a physical terrain.

Nina Wave, the skilled navigator and Network Security Specialist, took charge of deciphering the island's layout. Her keen analytical mind and extensive knowledge of network security were crucial in understanding the island's structure. "We need to get past these firewalls and access the central server," she explained. "But be careful—these systems are designed to detect and repel intruders."

As the crew ventured deeper into Cybersia, they encountered their first major obstacle: the Firewall of Fears. This formidable barrier was not just a physical obstacle but a series of advanced encryption algorithms designed to protect the island's most valuable secrets. Each layer of the firewall required a unique solution, challenging the crew's skills and adaptability.

Saul Ember, the Data Privacy Officer and Encryption Specialist, took on the task of bypassing the encryption. His methodical approach and precision were critical as he identified weaknesses in the algorithm, creating a path through the firewall. "Even the most secure systems have vulnerabilities," he noted. "It's all about finding and exploiting them carefully."

Here is a breakdown of the key measures Leo and his crew deployed in their battle to protect the Refineries:

Cybersecurity Measures:

- Firewalls and Intrusion Detection Systems (IDS): The crew established robust firewalls and IDS to detect and prevent unauthorized access to their systems. These defenses were their first line of protection against external threats.

- Encryption Techniques: To safeguard sensitive information, the crew used encryption techniques that ensured even if data were intercepted, it would remain unintelligible to anyone without the correct decryption key.

- Multi-Factor Authentication (MFA): For accessing critical systems, the crew implemented MFA, requiring multiple forms of verification, thus enhancing the security beyond simple passwords.

- Patch Management: The crew regularly updated their systems through patch management, fixing vulnerabilities that could be exploited by cybercriminals.

- Threat Intelligence: Utilizing threat intelligence, the crew stayed informed about the latest cyber threats, enabling them to pre-emptively guard against potential attacks.

Data Privacy Measures:

- Data Minimization: The crew practiced data minimization, ensuring they only collected and stored the necessary data to reduce the risk of exposure.

- Data Anonymization and Pseudonymization: To protect user privacy, they employed anonymization and pseudonymization techniques, making it difficult to trace data back to specific individuals.

- Data Access Controls: They enforced strict data access controls, ensuring that only authorized crew members could access sensitive information.

- Regular Audits and Compliance Checks: The crew conducted regular audits and compliance checks to ensure they adhered to data protection regulations and identified any areas needing improvement.

- User Education and Awareness: Finally, they prioritized user education and awareness, training each crew member on the importance of cybersecurity and data privacy, and how to recognize potential threats.

As they progressed, the crew encountered a series of puzzles and traps that tested their understanding of these principles. From phishing scams to malware attacks, each challenge was designed to simulate real-world cyber threats, giving the crew practical experience in handling various scenarios.

Ace Sharp, the Ethical Hacker and Cyber Defense Specialist, used his creativity to develop tools and solutions for overcoming these obstacles. His ingenuity proved invaluable in crafting devices to neutralize malware and secure their communications.

By the time they reached the core of the island, the crew was not only physically exhausted but also mentally stimulated. They had learned the importance of data encryption, secure communication channels, and the need for constant vigilance against cyber threats.

In the final moments of their journey through Cybersia, they encountered the Guardian of the Data Vault, a formidable entity responsible for protecting the island's most precious secrets. To gain access, the crew had to demonstrate their understanding of the principles they had learned throughout their adventure. They answered questions on data protection regulations, ethical hacking practices, and privacy laws.

With their knowledge and teamwork, the Digital Sentinels successfully proved their worth. The Guardian granted them access to the Data Vault, revealing not just the treasures of Cybersia but also the deeper understanding of data security and privacy they had gained. As they sailed away from the Isle of Cybersia, the crew reflected on their adventure. They realized that the digital world was as complex and dangerous as any physical realm they had faced. The lessons learned on this journey would be vital in their future quests, both in protecting their own information and in understanding the evolving landscape of cybersecurity.

"We've learned a lot on this adventure," Leo said, looking out at the horizon. "And there's still so much more to explore. But one thing's for sure—data security and privacy are just as important as any treasure we've ever sought."

The crew's journey through Cybersia marked the beginning of a new chapter in their adventures, one where the stakes were higher and the challenges more sophisticated. With newfound knowledge and skills, they were ready to face whatever the digital world threw their way.

13

# CHAPTER THREE: THE DATA PIRATES OF CLOUD ISLAND

After their enlightening journey through the Isle of Cybersia, the Digital Sentinels set their sights on their next destination: Cloud Island. Renowned across the digital seas for its advanced cloud infrastructure and thriving data marketplaces, Cloud Island was a hub of innovation and digital trade. However, beneath its glittering surface lurked threats that could undermine its very foundation.

As their ship sailed towards Cloud Island, the crew felt a palpable sense of anticipation. The island was a floating metropolis, its skyline dominated by towering data centers and sprawling networks that glowed with the constant flow of information. Cloud Island was not just a place of commerce but also a battleground where data pirates sought to exploit vulnerabilities for their gain.

Captain Leo Strong, ever the enthusiastic leader, addressed his crew with determination. "Alright, everyone! Cloud Island is full of opportunities, but we need to stay sharp. There are data pirates out there who want to steal and manipulate information. We're here to protect the integrity of this place and ensure that data remains secure and private."

Upon docking, the crew was greeted by Sky Captain Stratus, the island's vigilant protector and an expert in cloud security. Stratus explained the dire situation: a surge in data theft and sophisticated phishing schemes was threatening the stability of Cloud Island's ecosystem. The Data Pirates, a notorious group of cybercriminals, had been exploiting weaknesses in the cloud infrastructure to siphon off valuable data and disrupt services.

Nina Wave, the navigator and skilled Network Security Specialist, quickly assessed the situation. "We need to implement robust cybersecurity measures to safeguard the cloud systems. Let's start by strengthening the firewalls and setting up Intrusion Detection Systems (IDS) to monitor for any suspicious activity."

Here is a breakdown of the key measures Leo and his crew deployed in their battle to protect Cloud Island:

Cybersecurity Measures:

- Firewalls and Intrusion Detection Systems (IDS): The crew fortified Cloud Island's defenses by installing advanced firewalls and IDS to monitor and block unauthorized access attempts. These systems provided real-time alerts for any malicious activities.

- Encryption Techniques: To protect sensitive data, the crew employed strong encryption techniques, ensuring that even if data was intercepted, it remained unreadable without the proper decryption keys.

- Multi-Factor Authentication (MFA): They implemented MFA across all critical systems, adding an extra layer of security by requiring multiple forms of verification for access.

- Patch Management: Regular patch management was conducted to update software and fix vulnerabilities, preventing cybercriminals from exploiting outdated systems.

- Threat Intelligence: The crew utilized threat intelligence tools to stay informed about the latest cyber threats, allowing them to proactively defend against potential attacks.

Data Privacy Measures:

- Data Minimization: The crew practiced data minimization, collecting only the data necessary for operations, thereby reducing the risk of exposure.

- Data Anonymization and Pseudonymization: They applied anonymization and pseudonymization techniques to protect user identities, making it difficult for data pirates to trace information back to individuals.

- Data Access Controls: Strict data access controls were enforced, ensuring that only authorized personnel could access sensitive information.

- Regular Audits and Compliance Checks: The crew conducted regular audits and compliance checks to verify that all data protection measures were being followed and to identify any areas needing improvement.

- **User Education and Awareness:** They also focused on user education and awareness, training the island's inhabitants to recognize and avoid phishing attempts and other social engineering tactics.

Saul Ember and Ace Sharp, the crew's stalwart defenders, took on the responsibility of monitoring the network traffic for any signs of unauthorized access or data breaches. Their vigilance was crucial in identifying and mitigating threats before they could cause significant damage.

Meanwhile, Jack Forge and Flare Sky, collaborated to enhance the cloud infrastructure's resilience. Jack's inventive mind devised creative solutions to neutralize malware attacks, while Flare's engineering expertise ensured that the systems could recover swiftly from any disruptions.

Elara Deep and Riven Ash, leveraging their analytical skills, worked alongside Sky Captain Stratus to analyze the patterns of the Data Pirates' attacks. They uncovered that the pirates were using sophisticated phishing schemes to deceive users into revealing their credentials, which were then exploited to gain unauthorized access to the cloud systems.

As the crew delved deeper into the heart of Cloud Island, they discovered the Data Pirates' hidden operations center—a digital fortress fortified with multiple layers of security. To infiltrate it, the crew had to employ a combination of their cybersecurity and data privacy measures.

Nina led the charge in decrypting the encrypted data streams that shielded the pirates' communications. "We need to break through their encryption to understand their plans," she explained, her fingers flying over her digital interface as she worked to decode the messages.

Flare, ever the strategist, coordinated the team's efforts to deploy decoy data packets, distracting the pirates and diverting their attention away from the crew's true objectives. "While Nina works on the encryption, we need to keep them occupied," he instructed, ensuring that the Data Pirates remained preoccupied with the false leads.

Saul and Ace then moved to implement strict access controls, limiting the pirates' ability to move laterally within the cloud infrastructure. "If we can isolate their access points, we can contain their operations and prevent further data theft," Saul stated firmly.

Jack utilized his sharpshooting skills to launch targeted countermeasures against the pirates' malware, effectively neutralizing their attempts to disrupt the cloud systems. "Take that, you data thieves!" he exclaimed as he successfully dismantled a particularly nasty malware strain.

With the combined efforts of the crew, the Data Pirates' operations were systematically dismantled. Riven discovered a critical vulnerability in the pirates' phishing protocols, allowing the crew to trace the origin of their attacks back to a central command hub.

In the final confrontation, the Digital Sentinels faced off against Captain Phish, the leader of the Data Pirates. "You think you can outsmart us with your fancy cybersecurity tricks?" Captain Phish taunted, unleashing a barrage of digital assaults aimed at overwhelming the crew's defenses.

Leo, drawing upon the lessons learned in Cybersia, remained resolute. "We protect what's important, and we won't let you steal or manipulate our data!" With a powerful combination of multi-factor authentication and advanced encryption, the crew countered Captain Phish's attacks, ultimately forcing him to retreat.

With the Data Pirates defeated, Cloud Island's digital ecosystem was restored to its former glory. The crew's implementation of robust cybersecurity and data privacy measures not only protected the island but also strengthened its defenses against future threats.

As the Digital Sentinels sailed away from Cloud Island, they reflected on the critical importance of their mission. "Today we showed that with the right measures, we can protect even the most advanced systems from those who seek to exploit them," Nina remarked, a satisfied smile on her face.

"And it's not just about having the tools," Leo added. "It's about knowing how to use them and working together as a team."

The adventure on Cloud Island reinforced the crew's commitment to safeguarding data and privacy, setting the stage for the challenges that lay ahead. With each new island, they grew more adept at navigating the complex digital landscape, ready to defend the digital seas from those who threatened its integrity.

# CHAPTER FOUR: THE DEEP WEB DATAMINE

The victory at Cloud Island was hard-earned, but the Digital Sentinals knew their journey through the digital seas was far from over. Their next destination was a place shrouded in mystery and danger: the Deep Web Datamine. Unlike the bustling, vibrant islands they had visited before, the Datamine was a hidden realm beneath the surface of the internet, where secrets and shadows thrived.

As the Thousand Code navigated the eerie waters leading to the Datamine, the crew felt a growing sense of unease. The Datamine was notorious for harboring some of the most dangerous entities in the digital world—hackers, black market dealers, and rogue AIs, all operating beyond the reach of conventional cybersecurity measures. It was a place where data could be stolen, sold, or destroyed with little trace.

Captain Leo Strong, with his indomitable will, rallied his crew. "This place might be darker and more dangerous than anything we've faced, but we're not backing down. We're here to protect the innocent and stop those who misuse the power of data." His words filled the crew with determination as they prepared to descend into the depths of the Deep Web Datamine.

The entrance to the Datamine was a swirling vortex of dark code and fragmented data streams, a gateway to a labyrinthine network of hidden servers and encrypted vaults. As the crew plunged into this digital abyss, they were met with an overwhelming flood of information, much of it corrupted or deliberately misleading.

Nina Wave, the navigator and Network Security Specialist, quickly took charge, using her skills to chart a course through the Datamine's treacherous terrain. "We need to be careful. The data here is heavily encrypted, and there are traps everywhere—malware, spyware, and worse. We'll need to decrypt and analyze everything before we proceed."

Blade Zane and Ace Sharp worked together to create specialized countermeasures for the crew's journey. Zane designed a 'Digital Cloaking Device' to keep the Thousand Code hidden from the Datamine's prying eyes, while Ace deployed decoy data streams to mislead potential attackers. "We can't let them know we're here until it's too late," Ace muttered as he fine-tuned the decoys.

Raven Noir, with her sharp intellect and vast knowledge of information networks, began sifting through the data to find clues about their enemies. "We're looking for signs of illegal data harvesting and manipulation. The key players in the Datamine are masters of deception—they use deep fakes, misinformation campaigns, and other techniques to hide their tracks."

As the crew delved deeper, they encountered a series of formidable challenges. The Datamine was riddled with cryptic puzzles and seemingly unsolvable ciphers, designed to keep intruders out. These barriers were more than just digital—they were created using quantum encryption, a level of security that only the most advanced minds could hope to breach.

Steel Forge and Tide Force, the team's cyber defense engineers, found themselves up against rogue AIs programmed to defend the Datamine at all costs. These AIs were unlike any adversaries they had faced before—capable of adapting to their every move, learning from each attack, and countering with precision. "We need to outthink them," Steel grunted, dodging a barrage of digital attacks. "These things are like chess masters—they anticipate our every move."

Tide, always quick on his feet, responded by disrupting the AIs' communication channels, creating a temporary window for Steel to strike. "Even the smartest AI can't fight without data. If we cut off their access to the network, they're as good as blind," Tide explained, his eyes sharp with focus.

Chip Doc, the crew's Incident Response and Cyber Health Specialist, found his skills tested in new ways as well. The Datamine was filled with digital pathogens—viruses and worms designed to infect systems and corrupt data. Chip used his medical knowledge to identify these threats and developed antivirus solutions to protect the crew's systems. "These viruses are like diseases," he said, analyzing the code of a particularly virulent strain. "But every disease has a cure—we just need to find it."

The crew's progress through the Datamine was slow and perilous, but their efforts began to pay off when Raven uncovered a critical lead: a data packet containing information on a massive black market operation. This operation was led by a shadowy figure known only as 'The Broker,' a data trafficker who specialized in selling stolen information to the highest bidder.

Leo's resolve hardened as he learned of The Broker's activities. "We've got to take him down. He's not just stealing data—he's hurting people by selling their personal information to criminals." The crew knew that stopping The Broker wouldn't be easy; his network was vast, and his operations were deeply entrenched in the Datamine's structure.

With the information Raven had gathered, the crew formulated a plan to infiltrate The Broker's headquarters—a heavily fortified data vault hidden at the heart of the Datamine. The vault was protected by layers of quantum encryption, biometric locks, and a veritable army of rogue AIs. It was a fortress designed to be impenetrable.

Nina led the effort to bypass the vault's encryption, utilizing cutting-edge cryptographic techniques she had learned from her time on Cloud Island. "This is going to take everything we've got," she warned, her brow furrowed in concentration as she worked to decrypt the vault's defenses.

Meanwhile, Ace and Zane prepared the crew for the final assault. Ace designed specialized 'Data Bombs'— explosive packets of code that could disrupt the rogue AIs long enough for the crew to breach the vault. Zane, ever the defender, reinforced the Thousand Code's digital defenses to protect the crew from any retaliatory attacks.

As the crew made their way to the vault, they encountered The Broker's final line of defense: a massive AI construct known as 'The Guardian.' This AI was unlike anything they had faced before—it was self-aware, adaptive, and capable of controlling the entire Datamine's network. The Guardian's presence was overwhelming, its digital form towering over the crew as it unleashed a relentless assault.

Leo, refusing to back down, faced The Guardian head-on. "We're not going to let you or The Broker keep hurting people," he declared, his determination shining through. With the crew's support, Leo launched a coordinated attack, combining their skills and knowledge to exploit the Guardian's few weaknesses.

Steel and Tide worked in tandem, distracting the Guardian with feints and attacks while Nina and Raven focused on destabilizing its network connections. Ace's Data Bombs proved invaluable, disrupting the Guardian's attempts to repair itself and giving the crew the opening they needed.

In a decisive blow, Leo unleashed his full strength against the Guardian, shattering its core and bringing down The Broker's fortress. The crew rushed into the vault, where they confronted The Broker himself—a cold, calculating figure who had profited off the suffering of countless victims.

"Your reign ends here," Leo said, his voice filled with the weight of justice. The Broker, realizing he was defeated, attempted to escape, but the crew was prepared. With Nina's quick thinking, they locked down the vault, trapping The Broker and cutting off his access to the outside world.

With The Broker's operations dismantled and his data trafficking network exposed, the crew took control of the vault and secured the stolen data. Chip worked tirelessly to repair the damage done to the victims, helping to restore their stolen identities and erase the harmful data The Broker had sold.

As the crew emerged from the Datamine, they knew they had struck a significant blow against the dark forces lurking in the digital seas. The journey had been grueling, but it had also strengthened their resolve. "We're making the digital world safer, one battle at a time," Raven remarked as they sailed away, leaving the shattered remnants of The Broker's empire behind.

Leo, ever the optimist, grinned at his crew. "We're just getting started. There's still a lot of work to do, and we're the only ones who can do it."

With the Deep Web Datamine behind them, Captain Leo Strong and his crew set their course for their next adventure, knowing that even greater challenges awaited them on the horizon. But no matter what dangers lay ahead, they were ready—united by their mission to protect the digital world from those who would do it harm.

# CHAPTER FIVE: THE BATTLE FOR BLOCKCHAIN BAY

Captain Leo Strong's grand adventure leads him and the Digital Sentinels to Blockchain Bay, a renowned fortress in the digital seas where data transactions are secured by an unbreakable chain of blocks. In this bay, trust and transparency reign supreme, as blockchain technology ensures that all data is protected from tampering, fraud, and unauthorized access. Blockchain Bay has become a symbol of security in the digital world, where individuals and organizations alike rely on its robust defenses to safeguard their most valuable information.

The bay is not just a physical location but a beacon of hope for those who seek refuge from the chaos of the digital seas. Its walls are made up of the most advanced cryptographic protocols, and its waters are patrolled by vigilant security nodes that constantly monitor for any signs of intrusion. Blockchain Bay is a testament to the power of decentralized technology, where every participant plays a role in maintaining the integrity of the entire system.

However, this sanctuary of security has become the target of a formidable threat. The Forked Chain Gang, a group of elite cybercriminals led by the sinister Forkmaster, has set their sights on Blockchain Bay. Their plan is to exploit a critical vulnerability: the potential to create a "fork" in the blockchain. This split would allow them to alter the history of data transactions, rewrite the rules of the digital world, and establish a regime where they control all data flow—turning the digital seas into a realm of chaos and manipulation.

As the Digital Sentinels sail into Blockchain Bay, they are met by Ledger Lion, the bay's vigilant guardian and an expert in cybersecurity.

"Welcome to Blockchain Bay, Sentinels," Ledger Lion greeted them with a serious tone. "I'm afraid we're facing a grave threat. The Forked Chain Gang is targeting us, and they're trying to exploit a critical vulnerability in our blockchain."

Blade Zane's eyes narrowed in determination. "We're here to help. What do we need to do?"

Ledger Lion explained the gravity of the situation: the Forked Chain Gang has been systematically probing the bay's defenses, looking for weaknesses in its cryptographic protocols. "The gang has been deploying increasingly sophisticated attacks, including cryptographic exploits and social engineering tactics, to gather intelligence and prepare for their ultimate assault." If they succeed in creating the fork, they could compromise the entire system, leading to catastrophic breaches of data integrity and privacy.

Determined to protect Blockchain Bay, the Digital Sentinels prepare for a different kind of battle—one that requires not only physical strength but also a deep understanding of cybersecurity principles. The Forkmaster's plan involves launching sophisticated cyberattacks, including Distributed Denial of Service

(DDoS) assaults, phishing schemes, and advanced malware designed to disrupt the blockchain's operations.

The battle begins with the Forked Chain Gang deploying a massive DDoS attack, overwhelming Blockchain Bay's servers and attempting to shut down its defenses.

"Incoming attack!" Nina Wave shouted as the servers began to falter. "We need to reroute the traffic before we lose everything!"

Nina quickly assesses the situation, using her navigation skills to reroute traffic and prevent the system from crashing. She manipulates the network's flow, creating diversionary paths for the legitimate data to pass through while isolating and neutralizing the flood of harmful requests. Meanwhile, Ace Sharp and Steel Forge collaborate to enhance the bay's firewalls and intrusion detection systems.

"This is insane!" Ace exclaimed as he and Steel worked on fortifying the defenses. "We need to set up anomaly detection to handle this volume!"

"Already on it," Steel replied, his fingers flying over the keyboard. "We'll filter out the malicious traffic and keep the system running smoothly."

As the crew fends off wave after wave of attacks, Saul Ember and Chip Doc focus on identifying and neutralizing the malware embedded by the Forked Chain Gang.

"This malware is more complex than we thought," Saul said, studying the code. "It's embedded deeply within the system. We need to find the root of it and extract it before it spreads further."

Chip, leveraging his incident response expertise, coordinates a rapid containment strategy. "I'll isolate the compromised nodes and patch up the vulnerabilities," Chip said, his expression focused.

In the midst of this digital warfare, the Forkmaster makes his move to create the fork. He targets the blockchain's consensus mechanism, attempting to disrupt the process by which new blocks are validated and added to the chain.

"Time to make my move," Forkmaster's voice crackled through the communications system. "If I can disrupt the consensus, I can corrupt the entire blockchain!"

Tide Force, understanding the importance of defending the system's integrity, takes on the Forkmaster in a high-stakes confrontation. This is not just a battle of fists but a clash of minds, where every move has profound implications for the digital world's future.

But this battle is not just about brute force—it's also about securing the blockchain from the inside. With the help of Ledger Lion, the Sentinels learn to deploy advanced cryptographic techniques.

"To protect the blockchain, you need to understand its heart," Ledger Lion advised as he demonstrated the use of multi-signature verification and hash functions. "These techniques will help us ensure that the records remain tamper-proof and unaltered."

The Forkmaster unleashes his most potent weapon: a sophisticated ransomware that threatens to lock the entire system unless his demands are met.

"You think you've won?" Forkmaster taunted as the ransomware began encrypting the system. "Give me control, or I'll lock you out forever!"

Raven and Echo Strings lead the charge in breaking down the ransomware's encryption. "We need to crack this code before it's too late!" Raven said as she and Echo worked tirelessly. Nina and Ace, meanwhile, focus on mitigating the damage by setting up backup systems.

"We've got backup systems running," Nina confirmed. "Even if the primary blockchain is compromised, we can still recover critical data."

With time running out, the crew solves the final cryptographic puzzle, successfully preventing the fork and restoring the blockchain's integrity. Their victory is a testament to the power of collaboration and the unbreakable trust that forms the foundation of the blockchain.

The Forked Chain Gang is defeated, their cyberattacks thwarted, and Blockchain Bay is saved. "The blockchain remains unbroken," Leo said, relieved. "Our chain of trust and security is intact. We've made sure the digital seas remain a place where truth, transparency, and cybersecurity prevail."

# CHAPTER 6: THE TROJAN HORSE OF CYBER CITY

The Digital Sentinels find themselves in the heart of Cyber City, a sprawling, futuristic metropolis where digital life from all corners of the virtual world converges. Cyber City is a marvel of modern technology, built on the foundation of trust and transparency. Here, every citizen has access to vast amounts of data, stored and processed within the city's towering skyscrapers of code and algorithms. The city is protected by advanced cybersecurity measures, with firewalls acting as the digital walls and encrypted networks serving as the lifeblood of the city.

"Wow, this place is incredible!" Echo Strings exclaimed, eyes wide as he took in the towering digital structures and glowing data streams.

"It's a marvel of modern tech," Nina Wave said, adjusting her navigation instruments. "But something doesn't feel right. I sense a disturbance in the system."

However, this harmonious digital utopia is thrown into chaos when a mysterious Trojan Horse virus infiltrates the city's core systems. Disguised as a helpful application, this virus spreads rapidly through the city, corrupting everything it touches. Once trusted programs turn hostile, and the city's robust defenses begin to malfunction, threatening to turn Cyber City's once-safe environment into a dystopian nightmare.

"Alert! Security breach detected!" echoed a voice from the city's central control system, as screens across Cyber City flashed warnings of the Trojan Horse invasion.

The mastermind behind this cyber-attack is none other than Worm Lord, a notorious hacker and cybercriminal who thrives on chaos and control. Worm Lord's goal is to seize control of Cyber City by turning its own defenses against it, plunging the city into a state of perpetual fear and uncertainty. With the Trojan Horse virus as his weapon, Worm Lord plans to rewrite the city's digital laws, positioning himself as the ruler of Cyber City.

"Worm Lord, huh? We've got to stop him before he takes over this place," Captain Leo Strong declared, determination in his voice.

As news of the attack spreads, Captain Leo and his crew are called into action. They team up with Patch Panda, a skilled programmer and cybersecurity expert who knows the ins and outs of Cyber City's defenses. Patch Panda is determined to stop Worm Lord and restore the city's integrity, but he knows he can't do it alone. Together with Captain Leo and the Digital Sentinels, they embark on a mission to uncover Worm Lord's hidden lair and remove the Trojan Horse virus from the city's systems.

"I've been tracking Worm Lord's activities," Patch Panda explained, pulling up a digital map of the city. "He's hidden himself in the central server. We need to navigate through the corrupted areas and reach him before it's too late."

The journey through Cyber City is fraught with danger. The digital streets are now filled with corrupted code, and firewalls that once protected the city have been transformed into deadly traps. Blade Zane and Ace Sharp use their skills to cut through the corrupted programs that attack the crew, while Nina Wave uses her navigation skills to guide them through the city's complex networks, avoiding digital landmines and data traps set by Worm Lord.

"Watch out for those corrupted files!" Ace Sharp warned as he and Blade Zane slashed through a swarm of hostile data fragments. "These things are everywhere!"

As they delve deeper into the city, Raven Noir and Steel Forge work on deciphering the virus's code, trying to reverse-engineer its structure to understand its weaknesses. They discover that the virus has deeply embedded itself within the city's core systems, making it nearly impossible to remove without risking further damage. To make matters worse, Worm Lord has encrypted the virus with layers of malicious code, turning it into a formidable adversary.

"This encryption is like nothing I've seen before," Raven Noir said, furrowing her brow as she analyzed the code. "It's embedded deep within the system. We'll need a multi-layered approach to dismantle it."

In the final showdown, the crew reaches Worm Lord's lair, hidden deep within the city's central server—a massive, labyrinthine structure filled with traps and corrupted data. Captain Leo confronts Worm Lord, who has transformed himself into a powerful digital entity, capable of manipulating the city's systems at will. The battle is not just a physical confrontation but a clash of wills and intellects, where Captain Leo's strength and determination are matched against Worm Lord's cunning and control over the digital environment.

"Welcome to my domain, Digital Sentinels!" Worm Lord's voice boomed from the swirling vortex of corrupted data. "Let's see how you handle my Trojan Horse!"

Using his signature attacks, Captain Leo fights through the layers of corrupted code, each punch and kick representing a step towards restoring the city's integrity. Patch Panda assists by deploying countermeasures and decryption techniques, slowly unraveling the Trojan Horse's hold on the city. Meanwhile, Echo Strings and Brook provide support by distracting Worm Lord's digital minions, giving Captain Leo and Patch Panda the time they need to execute their plan.

"Leo, I'm almost through the final layers of encryption!" Patch Panda shouted over the din of the digital battle. "Just keep him occupied a little longer!"

In a climactic moment, Captain Leo unleashes a powerful attack that disrupts the virus's core, allowing Patch Panda to insert a final piece of clean code—a digital antidote that purges the Trojan Horse from Cyber City's systems. The city's defenses are restored, and the corrupted programs begin to heal, returning to their original, protective state.

"This is it!" Captain Leo yelled as he delivered the finishing blow to Worm Lord's digital form. "Let's finish this!"

With the Trojan Horse virus eradicated, Worm Lord's plans are foiled, and Cyber City is saved. The city's citizens, once living in fear of their own systems, regain their trust in the digital world. Cyber City once again becomes a beacon of trust and security, a shining example of how strong cybersecurity and data privacy can protect even the most advanced digital environment.

"We did it!" Patch Panda cheered as the city's systems began to stabilize. "Cyber City is safe once more."

"Good job, everyone," Captain Leo said, smiling at his crew. "We showed that Worm Lord that we don't back down from a fight."

# CHAPTER SEVEN: THE RANSOMWARE REBELLION

Captain Leo Strong's grand adventure leads him and the Digital Sentinels to Cryptoville, a once-vibrant and prosperous city known for its pioneering use of blockchain technology and cryptocurrency. As they approach the city, a cloud of darkness looms overhead, casting a shadow over the towering skyscrapers of code and algorithms that once gleamed with promise. Cryptoville had long been a hub of innovation and digital trade, where every transaction was secured by cutting-edge encryption and the city's infrastructure thrived on the secure flow of data.

But as the Digital Sentinels approach the city, they find it in a state of despair. The once-bustling digital avenues are now eerily silent, their vibrant lights dimmed. Cryptoville's skyline, once a symbol of technological triumph, now appears shrouded in a veil of corruption. The city's entire infrastructure—its power grid, communication networks, financial systems, and even the basic functions of daily life—has been locked down, encrypted by a malicious code that no one has been able to break. The attack has turned Cryptoville from a beacon of digital freedom into a city trapped in its own data.

"Look at this place," Leo mutters, his eyes scanning the devastated cityscape. "It was supposed to be a symbol of hope. Now it's just... a mess."

The mastermind behind this attack is none other than Crypto Croc, a notorious hacker who has made a name for himself in the darkest corners of the digital world. Crypto Croc, a shadowy figure in the digital realm, is known for his ruthless exploitation of vulnerabilities and his penchant for creating chaos. His name alone strikes fear into the hearts of cybersecurity experts. Crypto Croc demands an enormous ransom in cryptocurrency to release the city's data, holding the citizens of Cryptoville hostage in their own digital world. The citizens, once proud and independent, now find themselves desperate and helpless, unable to access their most basic needs without the approval of the hacker.

"This is bad, real bad," says Nina as she looks at the encrypted messages flashing on her screen. "We need to get to the bottom of this quickly."

As the situation grows increasingly dire, the citizens turn to the only group they believe can help—the Digital Sentinels. The city's desperation leads them to the docks where the crew disembarks, greeted by a team of frantic city officials. The crew is joined by Decryption Dog, a former cybersecurity expert who had once worked to protect the city's systems. However, disillusioned by the increasing power of hackers and the weakness of traditional defenses, Decryption Dog turned vigilante, fighting against digital threats outside the bounds of conventional law.

"Decryption Dog? I've heard of you," Leo says, extending a hand. "We're here to help. What's the situation?"

Decryption Dog, a grizzled figure with a deep knowledge of Cryptoville's systems, responds with a grim expression. "Crypto Croc has encrypted everything. The ransomware has locked down every critical system in the city. It's not just about the money; he wants control. If we don't act fast, Cryptoville will fall into chaos."

Upon entering Cryptoville, Leo and his crew are met with the enormity of the task ahead. The city's central hub, once a bustling center of digital activity, now appears as a chaotic whirlpool of corrupted data. The ransomware has encrypted every critical system in the city, and Crypto Croc has set up numerous traps to prevent anyone from attempting to unlock the data. Nina quickly realizes that the attack isn't just about the ransom—it's about control. By holding the city hostage, Crypto Croc aims to establish himself as a digital tyrant, using fear and coercion to dominate Cryptoville.

"We need to find the source of the infection and stop it before it spreads further," Nina declares, rallying the crew. "Steel, Ace, let's start by analyzing the city's infrastructure."

Steel and Ace begin by analyzing the city's infrastructure, identifying the points of entry the ransomware used to spread. They discover that Crypto Croc exploited a vulnerability in an outdated system that had been overlooked during the city's rapid growth—a critical lesson in the importance of regular updates and patch management in cybersecurity. As Steel works on patching the vulnerabilities, Ace sets up decoys and false trails to confuse the rogue AI defenders deployed by Crypto Croc.

"Look at this," Steel says, pointing to a broken piece of code. "Crypto Croc used this old vulnerability to plant the ransomware. We need to fix this before we can proceed."

Zane and Saul take on the role of defenders, physically confronting the corrupted programs that were once the guardians of Cryptoville but are now twisted into serving Crypto Croc's malicious purposes. Their battles are intense and relentless, as the corrupted programs have been transformed into formidable adversaries, attacking with a ferocity that reflects their new programming. They must overcome firewalls turned into physical barriers, and encrypted data blocks that manifest as impenetrable obstacles.

"These things just don't quit," Zane grunts as he slashes through a corrupted data block. "We need to keep pushing forward."

Raven and Chip work alongside Decryption Dog to analyze the ransomware's code. Their task is monumental as they face a web of encryption algorithms, each layer more complex and intertwined than the last. Raven's sharp intellect and Chip's precision enable them to identify weaknesses in the ransomware's structure. Decryption Dog, with his deep knowledge of Cryptoville's systems, provides insights into the specific coding practices Crypto Croc might have used, allowing the team to create a decryption key.

"This code is like a labyrinth," Raven explains as she deciphers the layers of encryption. "But I think we've found a way through."

As they progress, Leo and his crew find themselves in the heart of Cryptoville's central server, a massive digital fortress where Crypto Croc has taken refuge. The server is the city's brain, and Crypto Croc has fortified it with every trick in the hacker's playbook. Firewalls blaze with intensity, rogue AI defenders swarm like digital beasts, and the air crackles with the threat of corrupted data, creating a formidable battleground.

"This is it," Leo says, determination in his eyes. "We're going in. We need to end this now."

In the end, Leo confronts Crypto Croc directly, engaging in a high-stakes battle where every move could mean the difference between freedom and eternal digital enslavement for Cryptoville. Crypto Croc, confident in his control over the city's systems, underestimates the power of Leo's determination and the unity of his crew.

"You think you can stop me?" Crypto Croc taunts, his voice echoing through the digital realm. "This city is mine now!"

As the battle intensifies, Leo realizes that brute force alone won't crack the ransomware. Instead, he relies on the power of teamwork and the skills of his crew. Raven and Decryption Dog, working feverishly, finally manage to create a key that can bypass the ransomware's encryption. Nina uses her navigation skills to guide Leo through the treacherous server environment, avoiding digital traps and ensuring he reaches Crypto Croc's core without triggering any of the deadly failsafes.

"Leo, this way!" Nina directs as she navigates the complex server landscape. "We need to reach the core before it's too late!"

With no option left, Leo channels all his strength into a final attack that doesn't just destroy the ransomware—it purges the entire system of Crypto Croc's influence. The digital air hums with energy as Leo's powerful attack disrupts the core of the ransomware, creating a ripple effect that sweeps through the city's systems. The ransomware is cracked, and the city's systems begin to reboot. The locks on the city's infrastructure fall away, and Cryptoville is free once again.

"It's over, Crypto Croc!" Leo shouts as he delivers the final blow. "Your reign of terror ends here!"

With Crypto Croc defeated, the citizens of Cryptoville are finally free from the fear that had gripped their city. Leo and his crew teach them the importance of cybersecurity measures such as regular data backups, strong encryption, and awareness of phishing schemes and other social engineering tactics. They also emphasize the need for vigilance and preparation, reminding the citizens that the digital seas are full of threats, but with the right knowledge and tools, they can protect themselves from future attacks.

"Remember, this city's security is only as strong as its weakest link," Decryption Dog advises. "Stay vigilant and keep your systems updated."

As the Digital Sentinels sail away, Cryptoville begins to rebuild, stronger and more secure than ever. The city once again becomes a beacon of innovation and security in the digital world, thanks to the efforts of Leo, his crew, and their newfound ally, Decryption Dog.

"We did it, crew!" Leo exclaims with a broad smile. "Another city saved and another victory for us!"

The crew sails into the horizon, ready for their next adventure, leaving behind a city that has learned the value of resilience and the strength found in unity and preparedness.

# AFTERMATH

As the Digital Sentinels sail away from Cryptoville, the city begins its arduous journey to recovery. The once-paralyzed digital metropolis is now buzzing with activity as its citizens, guided by the lessons learned from their recent ordeal, work to rebuild their shattered infrastructure.

Leo, perched on the figurehead of the Thousand Sunny, gazes back at the city with a sense of accomplishment. "They've got a long road ahead, but at least they're on the right track," he says, his voice filled with optimism.

Nina, busy reviewing their next destination on the navigation charts, adds, "The citizens are working hard. They're already implementing new security measures and updating their systems. It's impressive how quickly they're bouncing back."

Steel and Ace, who had been instrumental in fixing the vulnerabilities, are now inspecting the ship's systems, ensuring they're in top shape for the next leg of their journey. "Can't believe we're leaving just as things are starting to look up," Steel says, giving a final check to the ship's controls.

Raven, alongside Chip and Decryption Dog, is finalizing a detailed report of their encounter with Crypto Croc. The report will serve as a guide for future digital defenses and strategies, ensuring that other cities can learn from Cryptoville's experience. Decryption Dog, with a contemplative expression, reviews the final lines of the report. "We've made a difference here. But this incident might just be the tip of the iceberg."

As night falls, the Data Sentinal crew gathers for a celebratory feast. The mood is buoyant, with laughter and camaraderie filling the air. Leo raises a toast, his eyes gleaming with pride. "To Cryptoville! And to us for saving the day!"

"To the Sentinals!" the crew cheers in unison.

But as the crew revels in their victory, a shadowy figure watches from the edge of the digital seas. A dark, cloaked silhouette stands on the shore, its eyes glowing with an eerie, malevolent light. The figure's presence is marked by an ominous crackle of static, hinting at its formidable power.

The figure steps forward, revealing a set of sophisticated cybernetic enhancements and a cold, calculating demeanour. In a voice laced with malice, it speaks into a hidden communication device. "The attack on Cryptoville was only a test. The real game is about to begin."

Meanwhile, back in Cryptoville, the city's central server room is abuzz with activity. The system is being carefully reconfigured and monitored to prevent any future threats. Amid the seemingly normal operations, a series of strange anomalies begin to appear on the monitoring screens.

"That's odd," one of the technicians mutters as they observe an unusual data spike. "It looks like there's some kind of interference."

The interference grows stronger, causing the screens to flicker and display cryptic messages. "Warning: Secondary Protocol Activated. Initiating System Lockdown." The message repeats, growing more urgent.

Decryption Dog, who has returned to the city for a follow-up inspection, receives an alert on his device. His eyes widen in alarm as he reads the message. "No way. This can't be happening. Not now."

He rushes to the central server room, where the technicians are scrambling to understand the issue. "What's going on?" he demands, his voice tense.

"We're getting encrypted signals," a technician replies. "It's like the ransomware's code is reactivating."

Decryption Dog's face turns grim as he realizes the implications. "We thought we had neutralized all the threats. This isn't just a random glitch. Someone's initiating a new attack."

As the crew celebrates, a chilling message appears on their communication devices. The message, encoded with sophisticated encryption, reads: "Congratulations on your victory. But you're not done yet. The real challenge awaits. —The Phantom Hacker."

The crew exchanges puzzled looks, their celebration abruptly halted by the ominous message. "Who's this Phantom Hacker?" Leo asks, his face set with determination. "And what do they want from us?"

The message provides a series of coordinates leading to an uncharted region of the digital seas. With their celebration cut short, the crew realizes they have no choice but to investigate this new threat.

Nina looks at the coordinates on her device, her expression shifting from confusion to concern. "These coordinates lead to a location that's completely off the map. We need to be cautious. This could be a trap."

"Whatever it is, we'll face it head-on," Leo declares, his resolve unwavering. "We've faced dangers before, and we'll face this one too. Let's set sail and find out what's really going on."

As the crew changes course towards the uncharted region, the crew prepares for what lies ahead. Decryption Dog, still in Cryptoville, watches the ship disappear into the horizon, his mind racing with the possibilities of the new threat.

"If the Phantom Hacker is behind this, then we're in for a serious fight," he says to himself, determination in his eyes. "I need to warn them before it's too late."

The scene shifts back to the shadowy figure by the shore. The figure's eyes gleam with a sinister satisfaction as it watches the Digital Sentinels set sail. The figure's lips curl into a cruel smile as they utter a final, chilling statement. "Let the games begin. This is just the beginning."

The screen fades to black, leaving the crew's next challenge shrouded in mystery and suspense.

www.ingramcontent.com/pod-product-compliance
Lightning Source LLC
Chambersburg PA
CBHW021143130726
47988CB00003B/1442